MONSTER APPETITE

Illustrated by Emi Ordás

fourth wall
publishing

There once was a boy called Henry
Who was well known for his greed.
Whenever his tummy rumbled,
He gobbled down food at speed.

A monster lived inside him,
And only poor Henry knew,
That when it started rumbling,
It wanted more to chew!

GRRRRRRr

One day Henry munched breakfast—
A giant pancake tower—
And then he stole his sister's!
Every crumb he did devour.

His parents screamed for him to stop,
He made his sister whine,
But Henry simply shrugged and said,
"It's the monster's fault, not mine."

The monster wasn't satisfied,
It wanted more to eat.
It made a menacing rumble,
"Give me another treat!"

When Henry took the bus to school
He spotted kids with lunch.
The monster began grumbling—
"Let me have a munch!"

So Henry ate the children's food
And emptied their lunch packs.
He quickly scoffed down everything,
From sandwiches to snacks!

His shocked friends looked at Henry
As he licked himself clean.
"It's just my belly monster–
It's not me being mean!"

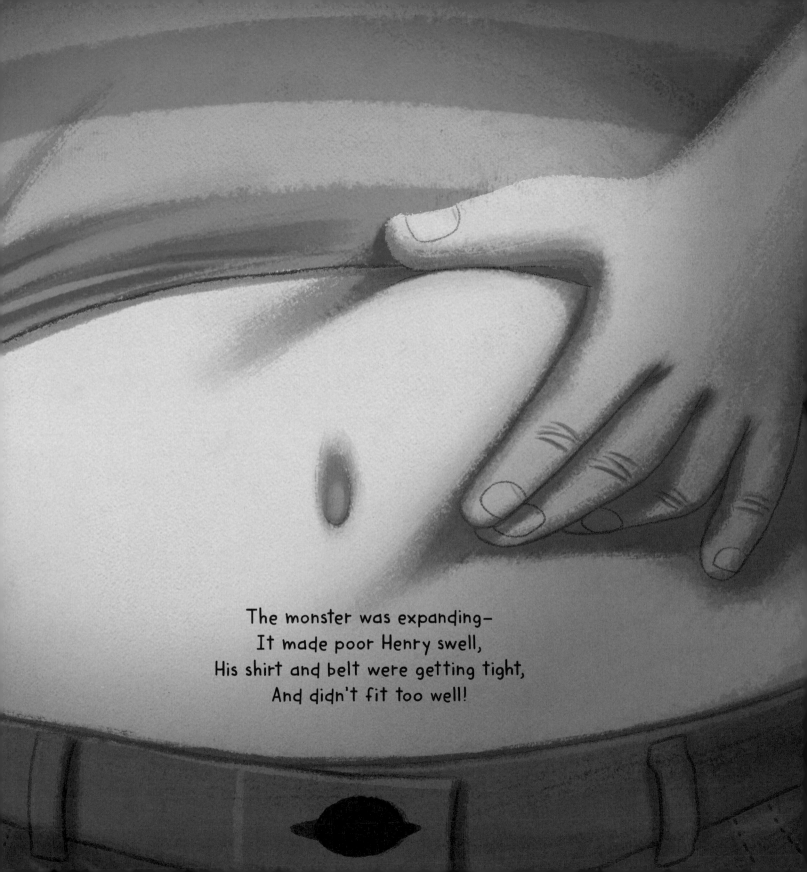

The monster was expanding—
It made poor Henry swell,
His shirt and belt were getting tight,
And didn't fit too well!

The next day in the classroom,
The smell of food crept in,
And Henry couldn't concentrate
With the monster deep within.

He sneaked into the canteen,
To find a mound of mash.
He grabbed a spoon and tucked right in—
It vanished in a flash!

He saw some sizzling sausages,
The monster made a 'ROAR!'
So Henry quickly swallowed them,
But the monster wanted more!

His classmates filled the Dining Hall
To watch Henry's last bite.
"But it's not me," he told his friends
"It's the monster's appetite!"

That afternoon, in cooking class,
Some treats were being made.
The smell was so delicious...
Henry's friends were all afraid!

Then Henry's tummy rumbled,
And let out a big moan...
The noise was growing louder,
It ended with a 'GROAN!'

Muffins, pastries, cakes and pies,
Henry ate the lot!
He emptied every baking tin
But it didn't hit the spot.

He looked at all his classmates
Who were upset and mad.
He'd eaten every bit of food,
And now was feeling bad.

But then Henry remembered,
That he should feel no shame,
"I don't decide to scoff the food—
The monster is to blame!"

Then, when school was over,
Henry walked home alone.
And as he reached his front door,
The monster gave a 'MOAN!'

GGGRRRR

So Henry grabbed a napkin,
And munched on meaty pies.
He gulped them down with gravy,
And a trough full of French fries!

No matter how much Henry ate,
Deep down the monster stirred,
Rumbling and a-grumbling,
He demanded to be heard!

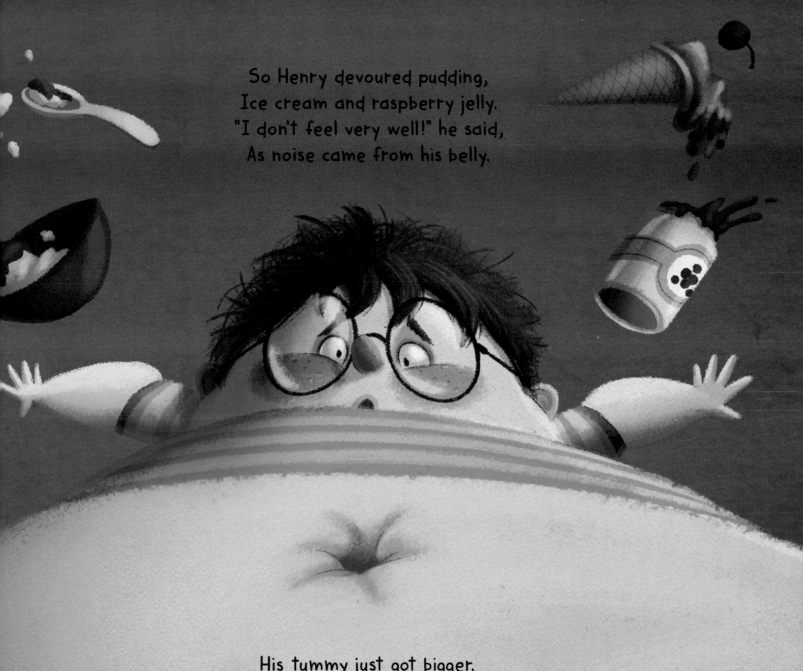

So Henry devoured pudding,
Ice cream and raspberry jelly.
"I don't feel very well!" he said,
As noise came from his belly.

His tummy just got bigger,
It wasn't going to stop.
His clothes were close to bursting—
Stand back! He's going to...

A strange, green, furry monster
Sat there in Henry's seat.
It looked at both his parents–
"Got anything else to eat?"

Something seemed familiar
About the monster's face...
Yes, Henry's little glasses
Didn't look too out of place!

When the monster spoke to them
Its voice sounded quite friendly.
So there was no surprise at all
When it said "My name's Henry!"

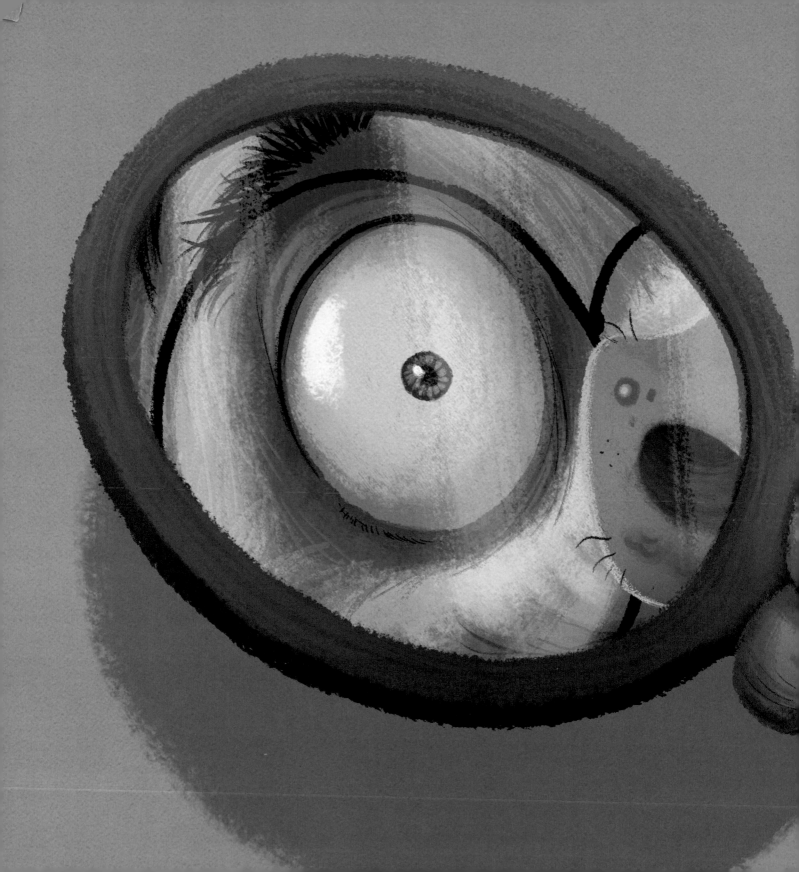

Henry gazed at the mirror
With shock as he could see—
A monster staring back at him...